SO-BVJ-512

AVE.
CALIF.

3 0050 01006 2932

ONE SEP   D

JUV PZ 7 .R288 Fam

Renick, Marion.

The famous forward pass pair

/

CAL-STATE UNIVERSITY, HAYWARD
LIBRARY

DEMCO

The Famous
Forward Pass Pair

illustrated by Charles Robinson

The Famous Forward Pass Pair

by Marion Renick

CHARLES SCRIBNER'S SONS
New York

JUV
PZ
7
R288
Fam

Text copyright © 1977 Marion Renick
Illustrations copyright © 1977 Charles Robinson

Library of Congress Cataloging in Publication Data
Renick, Marion.
    The famous forward pass pair.
    SUMMARY: Joe and Beeky resent Jan's interference in
their imaginary football games, but they find her point-
ers helpful when offered a chance for action on the
Bearcats team.
    [1. Football—Fiction]   I. Robinson, Charles,
1931-   II. Title.
PZ7.R288Fam   [Fic]   77-2943
ISBN 0-684-15037-9

This book published simultaneously in the
United States of America and in Canada—
Copyright under the Berne Convention
All rights reserved. No part of this book
may be reproduced in any form without the
permission of Charles Scribner's Sons.

1 3 5 7 9 11 13 15 17 19 MD/C 20 18 16 14 12 10 8 6 4 2

Printed in the United States of America

CAL-STATE UNIVERSITY, HAYWARD
LIBRARY

contents

one / The Secret Game

Beeky sat on the curb in front of his friend's house.

"Hey, Joe!" he called. "Come on out! Let's play football!"

Joe came and sat beside Beeky. He didn't bring his football. They didn't need one for their game.

"What team are we on today?" Beeky asked. "The Bearcats," said Joe. The Bearcats were boys from school. Joe and Beeky had this secret game of pretending they were Bearcats.

This time Joe started the game. "The Bearcats kick off," he said. "And the other team runs the ball back for a touchdown."

"That puts us 6 points behind right away!" Beeky didn't like that. He did what he could to stop the other team. "I block their kick. There! That keeps them from scoring the extra point."

7

"They kick off again . . . I think," said Joe.

"And I get the ball on our 30-yard line—" Beeky said.

Joe went on, "I run ahead and tackle a couple of guys."

"And I keep going . . . and going. . . . I'm halfway to their goal line and—" Beeky stopped.

Jan was coming across the street with a hop and a skip. She sang out, "What are you do-oo-ing?"

"Just sitting here," Joe answered. "Can't you see?"

He and Beeky looked at each other. That girl was always hanging around, trying to play with them. They wanted to keep their secret game to themselves.

But Jan had already caught onto it. She said, "Why don't you *really* play on a football team? You would have a lot more fun."

They told her to mind her own business. Jan made a face at them. She began to bounce her tennis ball on the sidewalk, counting ". . . nine . . . ten . . . eleven . . . twelve . . ."

Beeky and Joe went back to their secret game. They talked low, so she couldn't hear.

"Here comes a pass!" Joe pulled back his arm and pretended to throw. Beeky reached up and grabbed a handful of air. He stamped with his feet as if he were running fast. "Ho-HO! Touchdown!" he shouted, forgetting about Jan. "We're a famous passer and receiver! Sports writers call us the Famous Forward Pass Pair!"

"What sports writers?" Jan hooted.

They didn't hear her. Joe was saying their new name, trying it out. "The Famous Forward Pass Pair."

He and Beeky looked at each other. They liked it. They could see it already in big black letters in the newspaper. FAMOUS FORWARD PASS PAIR WINS FOR THE BEARCATS.

The Bearcats? That small-fry team of grade-school kids? Oh, no! Not famous players like Joe and Beeky. They would be the stars of the high school team.

From then on, in their secret game Joe always threw passes. They always whizzed as straight as arrows. Beeky always caught them with never a fumble. The Famous Forward Pass Pair won game after game for the high school team. It was easy without a football.

"Why don't you play with a real football?" Jan kept pestering them. One day she said, "My cousin Roger is the captain on a football team. He taught me how to play. Go get your football, Joe. I'll play with you."

"Oh, go bat your tennis ball," said Joe.

"On your own side of the street, too," said Beeky.

Jan did. But next day she was back again. She wouldn't let the boys play by themselves. She would start playing with her tennis ball in front of her house, then she would knock the ball over near them. When she came to get it, she would hang around. So she knew when they decided they were too good for the high school team. Next, she heard them talk about being on a college team. The week after that, they were playing in the Super Bowl.

"We're up against Texas," she heard Joe say. "The score is tied. They have the ball on our 20-yard line, and—"

"They fumble!" Beeky shouted. "They drop the ball and we get it! The crowd goes wild. *Put in the Forward Pass Pair!*"

"We run out on the field," Joe took up the tale. "We're in the huddle. I give the signal for a pass. *Hup!* You run way out to the side. Our team makes a pocket for me. I'm all set to throw. A Texas man breaks through. He rams his face guard into me. Ooof!" Joe grabbed his middle. "But I manage to get off a long pass."

"Two of their men race for the ball," Beeky went on. He was carried away with excitement. "I watch it coming . . . snatch it sideways . . . keep on running! They're right on top of me! But I make it to the 50-yard line. *Touchdown!*"

"Oh, fooey, Henry Beekman! You can't make a touchdown on the 50-yard line. That's the middle of the field." Jan laughed at him.

"What do you know about it?" he snapped.

"I know you aren't playing with a real football," she said. "I'll bet you don't even know how to catch one."

"That's what *you* think," Beeky said. "Go get your football, Joe. We'll show her some great forward passing."

"Yes, show me. Go get your football, Joe." She gave him a little shove. "Hurry up."

two /Jan Helps

Joe brought out his football. Jan said, "Don't just stand there with it. Throw it! Let's see Beeky catch it, like he says he does."

Joe and Beeky looked at each other. They had seen footballs thrown and caught in games on television. But they never had done it themselves. Joe tried to think of how to start.

"Go ahead. Throw a pass," Jan egged him on, "like in the Super Bowl."

Joe could not get out of it. He held the ball over his head with both hands. He called to Beeky, "Come a little closer."

Beeky took his time about moving.

Joe started again. This time he remembered to hold the ball with only one hand.

"Wait!" Beeky yelled. "There's somebody coming behind you."

"They're halfway down the block," Jan said. "You can throw a pass before they get near us."

Joe said he would rather wait. He turned around and saw a bunch of boys jogging toward him. They were swinging red football headgear. Their shoes clat-

tered on the sidewalk. Red letters on their gray warm-up shirts spelled *Bearcats*. In smaller letters below was *Junior City League*.

Joe just stood and looked. His dearest wish was to be in one of those gray sweat shirts, swinging his own red helmet. Beeky had the same wish.

Then Jan pranced right up to the Number 1 Bearcat and said, "Hi, Roger!"

"Hi, squirt!" He waved his hand. "I see you finally found somebody to play football with."

"She's not playing with *us*." Beeky spoke up.

"That's what *you* think," Jan said.

The Bearcats went jogging on by. She called, "Hey, Roger! Why don't you put these two on your team? Some people call them the Famous Forward Pass Pair."

Roger stopped. He turned back to take a look at Joe and Beeky. "We always need good players," he said. "You are kind of young. But if you're as good as my little cousin says . . . well . . . mmm . . . it wouldn't hurt to give you a try."

Joe and Beeky looked at each other. This might be their big chance. But could they make it with the Bearcats? They had just learned that the real thing is lots harder than make-believe.

"Wel-l-l," Joe began to back out.

"We're on our way to practice," Roger said. "You two can come along and we'll let you try out right now, if you want to." Beeky started away. Jan pulled him back.

Roger and his men started to move on. Joe and Beeky looked at each other. A couple of Bearcats yelled, "Come on, if you're coming!" Joe and Beeky hurried to catch up with them. Jan was right behind.

"See what I did for you?" she whispered in Joe's ear. "You're going to play with the Bearcats. Aren't you glad?"

Joe was not sure. One of the Bearcats asked, "What's your place in your team lineup?"

Jan made a quick answer. "Beeky catches the ball," she panted, out of breath from jogging. "And makes the . . . touchdowns. . . . Joe throws it to him."

Joe growled at her, "Go on home."

"No . . . we're almost to . . . the little park . . . where they practice."

Joe and Beeky jogged on. They couldn't bear to drop out—not with those red helmets bobbing around them! They gave each other a look that said, "Maybe we'll end up wearing one ourselves."

All they had to do was show how well they could play.

three/Jan Spoils
the Teamwork

The Bearcats began their practice. Roger told Joe and Beeky, "I'll put you in the lineup pretty soon."

"Will you put me in, too?" Jan asked. "Lots of teams have girl players."

"If these two friends of yours make it, I'll give you a chance," Roger promised.

In a little while, he called for Joe and Beeky. "How about trying one of your pass plays now?"

Joe was so excited he couldn't hold the ball long enough to throw it. Roger let him try over and over. Joe fumbled every time. Another player took the ball and passed to Beeky. Three times he did this, and Beeky missed every time.

"The Bearcats don't need fumblers," Roger said. "But we do need strong, tough linebackers. Suppose you try that."

Tissue paper. That's how strong Beeky and Joe were as linebackers. Roger looked around for his cousin. "Hey, Jan! Who told you these two are good players? Why did you—"

Jan was gone. Joe and Beeky were glad she didn't hear Roger say, "You don't even know what to do with a football. No team will have you till you learn how to play."

The boys didn't say much to each other on their way home. The next day after school they were sitting

on the curb again. As Beeky said, "Who cares about the Bearcats? We can still be the Famous Forward Pass Pair."

But that was not much fun any more. Not after they had almost been on a real team. Sure, they could still be superstars. But that was all talk. They wanted something better now.

One day Joe said, "I've been thinking. What if we really got good at our forward pass teamwork? Maybe—"

"Let's do it!" said Beeky. "Let's get so good that the Bearcats will beg us to be on their team."

So they began a new secret game. They played it with a real football. They only pretended, just a little, that they were star players.

Soon Jan came running. "What are you do-oo-ing?"

"Can't you see?" Beeky growled.

"I see you can't catch a football," she said.

"Joe throws too high." Beeky was always quick to make an excuse.

"No, he doesn't. You can catch it if you jump for it," she said. "I'll show you."

Joe threw again. Beeky reached for the ball but didn't touch it. Jan made a little jump and knocked it down. "That's how to do it," she said, pleased with herself.

Every time the ball came over, Jan outjumped Beeky. She crowed about it, too. Beeky and Joe looked at each other. They didn't say a word. They just stopped playing until she went home.

Jan didn't pester them for a few days. Beeky was now jumping for the ball like a circus poodle. Then Joe told him, "Don't just bat it down. Hold onto it."

"It wobbles too much," Beeky said. "I think there's something wrong with this ball."

When Jan came, he told her the same thing.

"That's no excuse," she said. "All footballs wobble. You have to know how to catch them." She turned to Joe and called, "Throw me a pass."

She made a neat catch. "See?" she crowed. "Do it like I do. Don't squeeze it."

Beeky snorted. Jan tossed the ball to Joe and called for another pass. She stood behind Beeky and said, "I'll show you again."

Beeky knew she expected him to let the ball go over

his head. He grinned to himself as he jumped for it. But it slid through his hands.

Jan got the ball. Beeky grunted, "What if you did catch it? You don't know what to do with it."

"I do so!" She held the ball under her arm and ran to Joe. "Touchdown!" she yelled. She laid it on the sidewalk. "Who-oo-ee! I made a touchdown!"

"That's the way to do it!" Joe shouted to his partner.

Beeky sniffed. Jan skipped back to her place behind him. "Let's do it again," she said.

Beeky went to Joe and said, "Let's stop playing until she goes away. She's spoiling our teamwork."

"Quit squawking, Beeky. *You* are spoiling our teamwork. You've got to learn to catch. Why don't you try harder?"

"She grabs the ball first."

"Beat her to it," Joe said. "Outjump her. Learn to hold onto the ball. Now, get back there and I'll throw straight to you."

Jan stood behind Beeky, waiting for the ball. He fooled her. He caught it. Then it popped out of his hands.

"I told you not to squeeze it," she said.

"Quit bugging me," he snapped.

"Come on, play ball!" Joe yelled at them. He started throwing passes. Jan stopped waiting for Beeky to miss one. She shoved in front of him to catch the ball. Then she would run to Joe with it, yelling, "Who-oo-ee! I made another touchdown!"

Beeky soon had enough. He stamped over to Joe. "I never get a chance to catch," he grumbled in a low voice. "We've got to make her leave us alone."

"Yep." Joe agreed. He thought it over. "How will we do it?"

"I know!" Beeky said. "We'll kidnap her."

four / The Police Come

"If we kidnap Jan, what will we do with her?" Joe asked Beeky.

"We'll hold her for ransom, of course."

"Who would pay any ransom for *her?*" Joe hooted. "Oh, I suppose her parents would. But we sure don't want to get mixed up with them. Maybe we'd better not do it."

"We won't really kidnap her. We'll only tell her that's what we're doing. And we'll let her go as soon as she pays the ransom. Don't you see?" Beeky asked. "We'll make her pay her own ransom. She will have to promise to let us play by ourselves."

"We won't hurt her, will we?" Joe asked. "We don't want to make her cry."

"We won't. She will only have to promise. Cross-her-heart-and-hope-to-die. Then we'll let her go. All we want is for her to stop spoiling our game."

"Maybe she is getting tired of that already. Maybe she will decide to play tennis instead of football." Joe thought about it, then said, "Let's give her another chance."

"Okay. But"—Beeky made a loud clap with his hands—"she gets kidnapped the first time she crows about grabbing the ball."

"She couldn't grab it if you got it first and held onto it. Why don't you try harder?"

Beeky pretended not to hear. But he began to catch more of Joe's passes. He even held onto some of them.

The next time Jan came bounding across the street, Beeky called out to Joe, "Remember what we're going to do!"

Joe yelled back, "Remember, we give her a chance first." He sent the ball spinning toward Beeky.

Jan jumped for it, grabbed it, and ran it back to Joe.

The boys looked at each other. Should they kidnap her now?

She settled it for them. She said to Joe, "I can catch better than Beeky. Why don't you throw to me instead of him?"

"Why can't all three of us play?" Joe asked. He was not sure what to do next.

"I've got an idea," Beeky said. "Let's go over on Ward Street and play. There's not much traffic there."

"That's a good place," Joe said at once. "We can spread out there."

"Come on, gang, let's go!" Beeky made the start.

Jan knew she should tell her mother where she was going. Yet she didn't want the boys to go off without her. When Joe said, "Come on, Jan," she went right along. But when they turned the corner to Ward Street, she stopped.

"I had better go home first," she said, "and tell—"

"Oh, no, you're not! You're staying with us." Beeky grabbed one of her arms. Joe took hold of the other. They started to pull her with them.

"Let go of me!" she yelled. "What are you do-oo-ing? *Stop it!*"

Beeky tried to tell her, "We're kidnapping you."

"We won't hurt you," Joe said. "Don't cry."

She wasn't going to cry. Not Jan!

She jerked herself loose, screaming bloody murder. She hit Beeky with her fist. He yelled. When Joe tried to grab her arm, she tripped him. As he fell, he got her by the leg. She reached for his shirt and tore it up the back. He let out a loud bellow. Beeky came behind Jan, grabbing hold of her shoulders. He tried to pull her back. She stamped on his foot. He howled with pain.

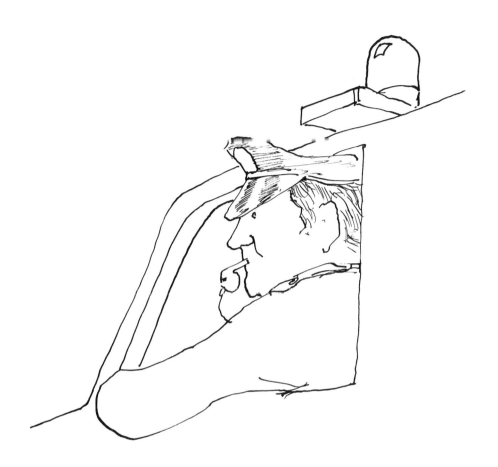

It was a wild, roaring, free-for-all scramble. It set the dogs barking for blocks around. No wonder the kids did not see the police car coming. The officer pulled to the curb beside them. He had to blow his whistle louder and louder before Jan and Beeky and Joe heard it.

That stopped them.

"What's going on here?" He looked them over.

Jan began to wail. "They're kidnapping me-ee-ee! They're dragging me off to some horrible place."

The boys had already let go of her. "No, we're not," they said in a hurry. "We're just playing."

Joe said, "We're only pretending to kidnap her."

"Yup." Beeky nodded. "We told her we wouldn't hurt her."

"They did so hurt me." She dangled her arms as if all the bones were broken. She looked pleased as she showed the officer. "See?"

"We didn't do that to your arms," Joe said.

"And you know it!" Beeky shouted.

The boys looked at each other. They were sure she was trying to get even with them.

"They dragged me, too. Look!" Jan stood on one foot to show the policeman her other shoe.

"Look how she tore my shirt!" Joe roared. And all three began yelling again.

By this time the officer was on the sidewalk. "Stop that racket! If you boys meant to harm this little girl, I can't drive off and leave her. Besides, you are certainly disturbing the peace. All of you. So get in the car."

They were very quiet now. The police officer got them into the back seat and shut the door. He locked it. Then he got in and drove off without another word.

five / The Little Red Card

Joe and Beeky were scared. They were sure the policeman was taking them to jail. Jan asked in a shaky little voice, "Where are we going, sir?"

"To meet some boys I know. They are the finest kids in town. They have something better to do than scare little girls. Or tear boys' shirts."

That didn't sound like jail. The three in the back seat began to breathe again. They felt even better when the officer stopped at a little park. They had been to this place before. And—just like that other time—the Bearcats were at practice.

Right away Roger spotted his cousin. "Jan! What are you doing in a police car?"

"Joe and Beeky tried to kidnap me," Jan answered.

"Why would they do *that?*"

"We didn't hurt her." Joe spoke up fast. "We only wanted her to stay out of our football game."

By this time, the whole Bearcat team had come to find out what was going on.

The officer smiled. "These two boys need the kind of help I gave you last summer. They need a team to play on. Would you let them come to practice with you? Maybe you could even use them on your scrub team."

"And me, too?" Jan asked. "I can catch better than Beeky."

Beeky started to say, "There she goes again—always butting in!" He remembered in time that Jan was Roger's cousin. Roger might turn against a boy who said that about her.

The policeman said, "Sure, let her try, too. She's a spunky little scrapper."

Roger asked his teammates, "How about it, guys?"

One said, "We already let these boys try out with us. They don't know beans about football."

But most of the Bearcats agreed. "Whatever Officer Benetti wants is okay with us."

Roger asked the policeman, "Do you have any more of those little red cards? The kind you gave us when we started the Bearcats? Those might help these kids to shape up."

"Who needs to shape up?" Jan asked.

"Read *that*, and you'll find out," said her cousin. He pointed to the small red card Officer Benetti was taking from his pocket. The policeman gave it to her. He brought out one for Joe and one for Beeky.

"Don't read it now," Officer Benetti told them. Opening the door of his police car, he said, "Hop in. I'll drive you kids back home. You can read your cards on the way."

"Mine says, *How to Make the Team*," Jan started to read out loud.

The boys looked at theirs. "Ours say the same thing," Joe said.

six / Where the Fun Is

"Our cards must be like yours," Joe said. "What else does yours say?"

Jan read it out loud:

> *"Learn how to play.*
> *Do your best. Keep on trying.*
> *Win without crowing,*
> *And lose without crying."*

Beeky said, "I don't see how that can help us make a team."

"Think it over," said the officer from behind the wheel. A few blocks farther on, he stopped to let them out. "Here you are! Back where I found you."

"Thank you. You're nice," Jan said. "I hope I see you again."

"You will. This neighborhood is my beat. I keep an eye on the Bearcats. So I'll keep an eye on you kids, too," the officer said. "And you keep your minds on what that little red card says."

Then he drove away.

"I want to show mine to my mom. Then she'll know where I've been." Jan hurried off.

Joe and Beeky sat on the curb reading the cards again. "It says, *Keep on trying*," Joe said. He looked around for his football. It was lying where they had dropped it when the kidnapping started.

Joe picked up the ball. "Let's go over to our street.
I'll throw you a pass on the way. Here it comes!"

Beeky caught the ball but dropped it. Joe shouted,
"Keep on trying!"

He began to try himself. He tried to make the ball
go a little farther and straighter each time. He and
Beeky worked at this for the next few days. They didn't

even mind having Jan try to break in and catch the ball. They just tried harder to keep it away from her. Joe said that was like playing against another team.

"When do you suppose we can start with the Bearcats?" Beeky asked. Joe wondered about that, too. Jan said she would ask Roger.

"He said for us to come this Saturday," she told the boys next day. "His team is going to play a team called the Dragons. He said we can sit on the bench. Like we are his second team. Some of the Bearcats can't be in the game that morning. One guy has to go to the dentist, and two others have to take a swimming lesson or something. So Roger will have only two extra players. He wants us there to make the Dragons think he has more than that."

"We won't fool them—not in these clothes." Joe looked down at his everyday pants.

"Oh, didn't I tell you? Roger is going to let us wear football suits from the boys who can't come," said Jan. "Won't we look neat? I wonder what number I'll have on my back?"

"You'd better wonder if the headgear will fit over your big head," said Beeky.

"Roger can make it fit," she said and turned her back on Beeky.

On Saturday Jan found out that Roger could not make her helmet fit. It kept wobbling. Her borrowed football pants didn't fit her either. She tied them around her waist with a shoestring. But the legs kept sliding down. Beeky's borrowed pants didn't fit him any better.

"Look how baggy they are!" he said. "I can't jump in these. I'll miss every pass I reach for."

"Listen to him crying about losing the ball!" Jan said to Joe. "And he isn't even going to be in the game."

Joe laughed. He asked Beeky, "Didn't you read that little red card the cop gave you?"

Everybody stopped talking to watch the Dragons
come into the park. "How many players do they have?"
Jan asked her cousin.

Roger looked worried. He was counting the new-comers: "... twenty-three ... twenty-four ... twenty-five. *Twenty-five!*"

The Bearcats never had more than sixteen players. And three of them could not be there this morning. Besides that, two more had bad colds. Roger had kept hoping they would show up. Now he knew they were not coming.

"We have only eleven men!" Roger rushed to tell Officer Benetti when the policeman arrived. "We don't have a chance to win."

"What if you do lose?" The officer looked at the boys one by one. He smiled. "The world won't come to an end. The main thing is to be in the game. That's where the fun is. To be *in* it, and to play your best."

"Remember that, you guys," said Roger. "Hang in there every minute. We don't have any more players to take your place."

"You've got *us*," Jan said. Nobody paid any attention.

seven / The Bearcats' Only Chance

The game started. Joe, Beeky, and Jan were too excited to sit on the bench. They were up at the sidelines cheering. "Stop him! Stop him!" they yelled when a Dragon started to run with the ball.

"Go! Go!" they screamed when the Bearcats had it.

At the end of the first half the score was Dragons, 0: Bearcats, 0.

"You are playing a whale of a game," Officer Benetti told the Bearcats.

They flopped on the ground around him. They were tired and out of breath. He had brought bottles of water. Jan helped pass them to the players.

"Is there anything we can do?" Roger asked the officer. "Every time we run with the ball, they stop us cold."

"A forward pass might work. It's our only chance. Why don't you try one?"

"Because we have only two men who can pass," Roger answered. "And they are both sick in bed."

Jan spoke up. "Joe is a good passer. He has been practicing hard."

Roger and Officer Benetti looked at the rest of the players. They all shook their heads.

One of the boys handed back an empty water bottle. "Thanks, Officer Benetti."

As the officer took the bottle he said to the boy, "What happened to your hand? It's bloody all over."

"Somebody stepped on it in that last play," the boy said.

Benetti felt the hand ever so carefully. "I think this calls for some first aid. You had better not go back in the game."

"Oh, no!" the boy groaned. So did everybody else.

"Now I bet you'll let Joe play," Jan said to Roger.

Roger looked miserable. "I guess we'll have to take a chance on you, Joe," he said.

Joe said, "I'm not going to play."

Jan blinked. "Joe! What's got into you? You know you want to play!" Joe only shook his head.

Roger didn't know what to do. At last he said to Jan, "You're a good scrapper. Go out there and—"

"Who-oo-ee!" She hitched up her football pants. She settled her red headgear. And into the game she went.

The second half started. The policeman stood beside Joe on the sidelines. He asked, "Why aren't you in this game? I know you want to play football."

Joe didn't answer. He just looked at the ground. Benetti put his arm around Joe. He said, "Tell me what the trouble is. Maybe I can help."

"You can't." Joe didn't look up.

"Don't be so sure, Joe. I want to see you in this game, throwing a pass. How about it?"

At last Joe said, "Not without Beeky to catch it for me. We always wanted to be football players *together*. We have our own passing teamwork. I don't want to go out there and leave Beeky just standing here."

"So that's it." Benetti gave him a pat. "Wait and see. Our boys are getting tired."

After a bit Roger called for time-out to give the Bearcats a little rest. Officer Benetti went onto the field to talk to Roger. Then Roger sent two players to the bench. He crooked his finger at Joe and Beeky.

The Famous Forward Pass Pair looked at each other. They were kind of scared. But in a way this was old stuff to them. They trotted onto the field.

Roger put Joe in at quarterback. He told him what number to call for a pass play.

"Got that, Beeky?" Joe asked. Beeky was to play end. He swallowed hard and said, "Yup."

"Now it's up to you two," Roger said. "I'm at center. I'll be very careful when I shove the ball back to you, Joe."

eight/Roger Says "Someday"

The teams lined up. Joe knew how a quarterback calls
signals. He stands with one hand on the center's back.
Joe knew how a quarterback bends down to take the ball
from the center. It looked easy.

IIe tried it— and dropped the ball.

Jan pounced on it. "I kept the Dragons from getting it," she crowed.

The Bearcats tried again. Joe got the ball safe in his hands. He stood tall to look for Beeky. He waited too long to throw. The other team mowed him down. They got the ball.

"Where were you?" he asked Beeky. "You were supposed to run out to the side."

"I had mud on my shoes. I couldn't run fast."

Joe gave him a look.

All the Bearcats tried hard. But the Dragons had the ball. They soon made a touchdown. But they missed the kick for the extra point. The score was Dragons, 6: Bearcats, 0.

Joe and Beeky were afraid they would be sent to the sidelines. But Roger said, "Our only hope is to keep trying passes. You two might just make one good for a touchdown."

The Bearcats did get their touchdown. Roger made it. The Dragons dropped the ball. He grabbed it and ran with it. Now the teams were even. Dragons, 6: Bearcats, 6.

"Let's get that point after touchdown!" Roger told his team. "Oh, gosh—we don't have our kicker today."

Roger chose a boy to make the kick. He told Jan to hold the ball for him. She asked the kicker how she should do it.

"I don't know. I never kicked before," he said.

She was sure his kick was not going to win that extra point. Then she remembered something as the teams lined up. Officer Benetti had said their only chance was a forward pass.

"Pass, Joe! Pass! Pass!" she screamed. Just then the ball came into Joe's hands.

Without thinking, he yelled, "Beeky!" And he threw the ball as hard as he could.

Beeky knew where he was supposed to catch it. He and Joe had done this many times. The Dragons were expecting a kick. They were too surprised to stop Beeky as he tore around them. The ball was in the air. He ran on, watching it over his shoulder. He didn't even have to jump for it. It floated down into his reaching hands. With one more step, he crossed the goal line. The game ended, Bearcats, 7: Dragons, 6.

The Bearcats were proud of Joe and Beeky, and they said so. Roger told them, "We can use a forward pass pair like you again someday."

"It was me who called for a pass," Jan reminded him.

"I wondered why you did," he said. "You don't know that much about football."

"Maybe I know more about football than you think I do."

"And you're always crowing about it, too. Go read your little red card again," said Beeky. Then he added some kinder words. "But you're a real good football player, anyway."

"I'll say you are!" Roger turned to her. "You can play with this team any time you want to."

Joe and Beeky looked at each other. They wished Roger had said that to them. Still, he had said, "Someday." They felt good as they took off their borrowed football suits. Someday they would have their own.

Jan had already jerked off her red headgear. She was tired of that heavy thing wobbling on her head. She was tired of pulling up those ugly brown football pants.

From that day on, Joe and Beeky thought only of football. They never missed watching the Bearcats practice. They themselves practiced at home until it was too dark to see the ball. They got better and better at their teamwork. This was their secret game now.

Once in a while they said to each other, "We're going to be a Famous Forward Pass Pair someday."

Jan would see them busy at their game. But she did not rush over to join in. She was too busy slamming a tennis ball against the garage door. Again and again and again, she would try to hit it back with her racquet. She was playing a secret game of her own.